MR. NOSEY

by Roger Hargreaves

PSS!
PRICE STERN SLOAN

Mr. Nosey liked to know about everything that was going on.

He was always poking his nose into other people's business.

Mr. Nosey was the kind of a person who, if they came upon a locked door, couldn't resist looking through the keyhole to see why the door had been locked.

Mr. Nosey was the kind of a person who, if he found an unopened letter addressed to somebody else, would simply have to open it to find out what was inside.

Mr. Nosey was the kind of a person who, if he was sitting reading his paper on a train, would much rather read the paper of the person sitting next to him.

Naturally, as you can imagine, Mr. Nosey was not very popular.

People did not like the way in which Mr. Nosey would peek and pry into their affairs.

They did not like it at all, but did that stop Mr. Nosey from peeking and prying?

It did not!

Mr. Nosey lived in a place called Tiddletown.

One day, the people of Tiddletown decided that Mr. Nosey was becoming much too nosey, and so they held a meeting to discuss what to do about him.

"We must find some way to stop him from being so nosey," said old Mr. Chips, the town carpenter.

"That's right!" said Mrs. Washer, who ran the Tiddletown laundry. "He needs to be taught a lesson."

"If only we could think of a way to stop him poking his nose into everything," said Mr. Brush, the painter.

And then, a small smile spread over his face.

"Listen," he said, now grinning. "I have a plan!"

All his friends gathered around to listen to his plan.

The following morning Mr. Nosey was out walking along High Street in Tiddletown when he heard somebody whistling behind one of the closed doors.

"I wonder what's going on here?" he thought to himself, and tiptoeing up to the door, he quietly opened it and peeped in.

"SPLASH" went a very wet paint brush right on the end of Mr. Nosey's nose, covering it with bright red paint.

"Oh dear. I AM sorry!" said Mr. Brush, who was painting the inside of the door.

Poor Mr. Nosey had to go straight home to try and remove the red paint, which was very difficult and rather painful.

Mr. Brush chuckled to himself.

The Plan had begun.

The following day Mr. Nosey was walking past the laundry when he heard somebody laughing on the other side of the wall.

"I wonder what's going on here?" he thought to himself, and standing on tiptoe he looked over the wall.

"SNAP" went a clothespin right on the end of Mr. Nosey's nose.

"Oh dear. I AM sorry!" said Mrs. Washer, who was hanging up clothes on a washing line on the other side of the wall.

Poor Mr. Nosey removed the clothespin, and went off down the street feeling extremely sorry for himself and for his poor red nose.

Mrs. Washer chuckled to herself.

The Plan was working.

The next day Mr. Nosey was going past a fence when he heard hammering.

"I wonder what's going on here?" he thought to himself, and creeping very quietly to the end of the fence, he peeped around.

"BANG" went a hammer right on the end of Mr. Nosey's nose.

"Oh dear. I AM sorry!" said old Mr. Chips, who was nailing up a loose plank in the fence.

Poor Mr. Nosey had to go home immediately and bandage his poor red sore nose.

Mr. Chips grinned a broad grim.

The Plan was working very well indeed.

The following day Mr. Nosey was walking in the woods when he heard somebody sawing wood.

"I wonder what's going on here?" he thought to himself, and he crept up behind a tree.

He was just about to peer out from behind the tree when it suddenly occurred to him that if he did, something very nasty might happen to his nose.

And so, he went on his way without being nosey.

Behind the tree, with a saw raised in his hand, stood Mr. Herd the farmer.

When he saw that Mr. Nosey had gone on his way without being nosey he laughed and laughed and laughed.

The Plan had worked.

Mr. Herd hurried into Tiddletown to tell everybody.

The Plan really had worked because after that Mr. Nosey stopped being nosey and soon became very good friends with everybody in Tiddletown.

And that is the end of the story, except to say that if you are ever tempted to be as nosey as Mr. Nosey used to be, you'd better expect one thing.

A sore nose!